WHY THE SECRETS

ATHALIA MONAE

Why the Secrets

Copyright © 2019 by Athalia Monae

Acknowledgments

I thank my higher power for being my guidance and for blessing me with opportunities where I'm able to use my talents.

My sincere thanks to my editor, Howard Rankin, who not only did the editing but also graciously gave me great advice.

For those who read my short story and enjoyed it so much that you continuously asked me to write more, I appreciate you.

Thank you to my family members who has supported and encouraged me on this journey. Love you all!

Blessed Beyond Measure

TABLE OF CONTENTS

WHY THE SECRETS

Queen Jones is the nine year old daughter of a successful African American married couple. She and her parents were very close with each other, as well as with their extended family.

That all changed one day when Queen woke up expecting to see her father, Charles, as she had always, but this time he wasn't there.

She immediately started asking her mom, Linda, questions about her father's whereabouts and continued to do so as she got older, but her mom always avoided answering. Fast forward a decade later. Queen is now a college student and her mom is remarried to a successful white man, but Queen still hasn't received an explanation for her father's disappearance.

As a result of a horrible accident, the shocking truth comes out about everything. Even the reason as to why she and her mom no longer had a relationship with some of their extended family and why they had never met Queen's mom new husband, Mark. Queen is so stunned regarding the reason for her father no longer being a part of her life that she starts to search for him; she has to hear his side of the story. She eventually finds her father in the most unexpected way.

The intriguing insight as to how one family secret caused a domino effect of pain and stress.

Will there ever be an end to the family drama?

WHAT COULD BE SO BAD?

Queen looked at the calendar, "December 19, 2015. Yes! One more week until Grandma Beatrice's visit," thought Queen. Her mom had given her the perfect name, because for as long as she could remember, she had always been treated like a queen. She had the best quality of everything, including education; she even received a brand new BMW for her 18th birthday. Queen was very popular in high school and even in college.

Queen Simone Jones would be graduating from college in the spring of 2016. She was so excited about that, but she was even more excited knowing that she would soon be getting her annual Christmas visit from her grandmother. After all, Grandma Beatrice, Aunt Connie,

Uncle Mike and Cousin Monique were the only family members that Queen had a relationship with. Grandma Beatrice is the mother of Queen's mother Linda, Connie is Linda's younger sister, Uncle Mike is Connie's husband and Monique is their daughter. Grandpa James and Uncle James, Jr., never visited Queen and Linda and vice versa. Queen's father, who was the number-one man in her life, was here one day and the next he was gone. That was very weird because she, her mom and her dad had such a special and loving relationship. Queen never knew why her dad suddenly stopped coming home and trying to find out from her mom was like pulling teeth. The first time she asked her mom about it, it seemed like it was a painful question. Her mom only told her that it was complicated. She accepted her mom's explanation because she didn't want to hurt her mom by asking her to explain.

Although Queen lived this wonderful life, she was very humble and grounded; Linda wouldn't have it any other way. She tried to make sure that Queen had everything that she needed and mostly what she wanted. Queen was given so much, but she wasn't given the one thing that she longed for, she wanted to know the truth about her non-existent relationship with her family and the disappearance of her dad.

The reaction that Queen got from her mom after questioning why Grandpa James and Uncle James Jr. and his family never visited was the same type of reaction she would receive when she asked about her dad, whom she hadn't seen nor talked to in about 14 or 15 years.

"Hey Momma, where's daddy? He's late again. Is daddy ever coming back home?" Queen could remember asking her mom these questions continuously when she was younger. She asked her mom numerous questions after she noticed her dad not coming home night after night. That was very strange because previously Queen's dad would come home every evening, shortly after Queen and her mom would arrive home. She was daddy's little girl.

Her mom bent down and kissed her on the forehead and said to her, "Little Queenie, your daddy had to move on but we are going to be okay, I promise you."

When the little girl looked up at her mom, she noticed tears in her eyes.

"Momma aren't we still going to be Momma, daddy and Queenie?"

"No baby, just Momma and Queenie."

Queen sat staring out of her bedroom window thinking about that very confusing day, when she was younger. She decided to give her grandma Beatrice a phone call and ask her the questions that her mom had avoided answering for so many years. Grandma Beatrice was Queens's second best friend after Linda. Queen loved how much of a straight shooter grandma Beatrice was. She was not to be played with.

"Hello grandma Beatrice, how are you?"

"I'm fine Queenie, how are things going with you?"

"Just great grandma, I'm singing a solo in church this Sunday. I'm a little nervous, but I will be fine. How are Grandpa James and everyone else doing?

"Everyone is fine baby, just fine."

"Hey grandma!"

"Yes baby?"

"I have something I would like to ask you. All I ask is that you're honest with me, just like you are about everything else."

"Sure baby, what's going on? Talk to me chile."

"Okay, first of all, where's my family? Why is it that you, Aunt Connie and Aunt Connie's family is the only family members that comes to visit Momma and me? Why is that me, mom and Mark never visit you all?"

Mark Baskin is Linda's white husband of nine years.

"What happened to my daddy?"

Although Queen still missed her father after all these years and felt the need to know what was behind the reason for her not having him in her life anymore, she still loved and appreciated Mark. He was a wonderful stepfather to her. He and his family welcomed her and Linda into their family and loved them unconditionally. Their family was everything that Queen wished hers was. They supported each other in every endeavor. They celebrated everything together from an elementary school graduation to the birth of a new baby. When one hurts, it seems to affect them all, and they all got through it together. Now that's love.

From Queen's younger childhood she remembers her own family being so close. What could have gone so wrong that would separate her family so drastically? Queen thought to herself.

There was silence on the other end of the phone.

"GRANDMA BEATRICE, GRANDMA?"

"Yeah! Yeah! I'm still here chile, stop yelling. Um, Queenie look here baby, grandma has never lied to you and I'm not about to start now. Please forgive me, but these questions are not for me to answer. Talk to your momma about this. You definitely deserve to have these questions answered."

"Grandma, do you realize the last time I saw my daddy I was seven years old?"

"Yes I do baby and I'm sorry for you," grandma said.

"I have memories of my daddy bathing me, cooking dinner for me, him and mom. I remember the three of us going to the park together, as a family. I remember seeing him and mom kissing each other, and then all of a sudden he's gone, just like that. I've never seen him again. Grandma Beatrice I am not a child anymore, I'm an adult and whatever the truth is I can handle it.

I had Grandpa James, Uncle James Jr., Aunt Jackie

and my cousins Stacey and Trina, now they're all gone, too. This makes no sense to me and no one's trying to make any sense of it for me. I feel like I'm being treated like a porcelain doll that will crack at the sound of truth and reality. I guess you all don't realize just how strong I am. I'm neither weak nor fragile; I'm a strong black woman."

"Queenie, listen to me."

"Yes ma'am." Queen said.

"Talk to your Momma."

"Grandma, I've already tried talking to her to try and get my questions answered, but nothing. This is a very emotional subject for her and I really would like to know why."

"I know that you've already tried talking to her, but try again and this time don't give up. Grandma loves you, don't ever forget that."

"I love you too grandma."

A BLESSING IN DISGUISE

Mark was out of town on business. Whenever he and Linda were apart they missed each other so much that they would schedule times to call each other every day. Between the two of them, they would call about 3 to 4 times per day. For the past several months they had been working on trying to have a baby. It would be Mark's first child. They were both excited about the possibility of having a child together. Working on conceiving was something they had been putting off because both of their careers were booming.

It was two days before Christmas. Linda and Queen were trying to run all their errands early because Mark would be returning home that evening from his business trip and they wanted to have dinner together as a family. Also, the following morning they would have to pick Grandma Beatrice, Aunt Connie and her family up from Los Angeles International Airport. There was still so much to be done. Christmas was Queens's favorite holiday but having her grandmother, aunt, uncle and cousin there made it even better.

They needed to shop for a new Christmas tree and, of course, new ornaments. They hadn't bought any gifts yet, not even one. Queen wanted to confront her mom again about her almost empty family tree, but she didn't know how to go about it this time. *Is it even worth it?* She thought to herself. "Mom, since we're almost finished with everything let's stop at the mall to get some ice cream, it's been awhile since we've done that."

"Sounds good to me, you might as well sit on Santa's lap and tell him what you want for Christmas babe."

"Oh! What a good idea mommy. Maybe, just maybe, I will get what I've wanted for so long." Queen said. Linda laughed. It was funny Queen thought, but if she could seriously ask Santa all the questions her mother keeps avoiding and get the answers, that would be great.

Just then Linda's cell phone rang.

"Well hello Ms. Stacey, how are you?"

Stacey? Why would Stacey be calling us after all these years? Queen thought. Something must be wrong.

Stacey is Uncle James's daughter. Just then Linda started stuttering.

"Wait, wait, calm down and start all over again baby. Uh! Huh! Okay!"

Queen stood staring at her mom, who looked like she was about to go into shock.

"Stacey, let aunty call you back. Okay, we love you too."

"Mom is Uncle James okay?" Queenie asked her mom. "What's going on mom?"

"Uncle James is fine Queen."

"Then what's wrong, who is it?"

"It's your grandmother, she was in a car accident this morning and she's hurt pretty badly." "Momma we have to go see about her."

"We are going to see about her Queen. You, Me, and Mark will go see about Momma."

Queen liked the sound of that. Besides Grandma Beatrice, Aunt Connie and Aunt Connie's family, Mark had never met any of Linda's other family members.

Linda and Queen met Mark at the airport with packed suitcases and brought him up to speed about the car accident. They arrived in Detroit, Michigan at 9:30 p.m., checked into the hotel and headed for the hospital.

"Baby call the hospital before we head over there because I'm almost positive visiting hours ended already," Mark said to Linda.

"Yeah, you're right babe."

"Mom let's check on Grandpa James to find out how he's doing and to get an update on Grandma." said Queen.

John, Linda and Queen arrived at Grandma Beatrice's house, where the rest of the family had gathered.

Everyone was so happy to see Queen and Linda. Although Aunt Connie and her family and Grandma Beatrice, were the only family to have ever met Mark, he was still greeted by everyone else as if they knew him already. It made Queen and Linda both happy to see how their family greeted Mark. Queen noticed how everyone except Uncle James happily greeted her mom and Mark. Uncle James just stood there scowling. Queen walked up to her uncle, wrapped her arms around his neck and gave him a big kiss. James couldn't help but to smile and return the hug and kiss to his niece.

BRIDGING GAPS

"It's nice of you to come and see about our mother instead of the other way around," James snarled at Linda.

"Why wouldn't I come to see about our mother, James?" Linda said.

Connie angrily stared at James.

"Not now James, this is not the time for your mess," Connie told him.

Queen stood there in disbelief. She knew that her mom's relationship with certain members of her family was strained, but she still couldn't believe what she was witnessing.

"What's going on? I'M SICK OF THIS ALREADY," Queen shouted.

Everyone stood in silence.

"Linda if you would like to talk to your daughter, you all can go into Momma and Daddy's bedroom for some privacy."

"PRIVACY, she don't need any privacy Connie," James shouted.

"Queenie, your mother took you from your daddy and tried to replace him with a white man, and that is unacceptable to me, that's what's going on."

"James, keep your mouth shut and mind your business," Connie shouted. Linda's father had similar feelings as James Jr., but he would never disrespect Mark and Linda, how James Jr. had.

Linda stood crying.

"James are you that hateful that you don't have any compassion for anyone? I don't remember you ever congratulating me for putting myself through law school and being a successful attorney. I don't remember you ever congratulating me on raising your niece to be the smart, intelligent and selfless young woman that stands before you right now. Since I've moved away, you've never, not once, returned any of my phone calls when I called to check on you and your family, but you will stand here and point out the fact that I'm married to a white man. Not only is that disrespectful to both he and I, but it is very ignorant and hurtful."

"James, since you don't know anything about the man that you just stood here and disrespected, let me tell you a few things about him. Mark is my best friend. He has been nothing but good to Queen and me. He supports us in everything we do. He encourages us, he listens to us. He's there for us on our good days as well as our bad days. Mark respects me emotionally, physically and mentally. He LOVES us. These are only a few of the things about Mark. What does it matter what color he is? ANSWER ME JAMES."

James was silent. "Charles was good to you too Linda. He loved you and Queen. He was a good provider and supporter. He was a wonderful father and a damn good husband. You took his daughter and just left."

"James stop for a minute, just stop. You say I took Charles daughter and just left. You're my brother; we were raised in the same household, by the same parents.

Didn't you think that that was out of character for me to just leave? You know how close I was to our family. You know how much of a family person I am. Knowing this, you never questioned me why I just left. It was more convenient for you to hold a grudge against me and to disrespect a man you know nothing about. James I thought that you were better than that, but it looks like we don't know each other very well after all."

"Linda I will wait for you at the hotel. Call me when you all are ready and I will come to pick you up," Mark said. "Mark, wait a minute baby. You, me and Queen will leave together."

Connie and Grandpa James apologized to Mark for James outburst. Grandpa told James to take his family and to go home. Connie kissed her father on the forehead, "thank you daddy."

"No daddy let him stay," Linda demanded.

"Queen first of all I want to apologize to you for letting so much time go by without explaining things to you. I know that you remember the happy family that we had together with your father, and those were some happy times. Shortly after your dad became a lawyer, he started to change. Some change was for the better and some was not, namely his professional peers. He started having late meetings one to two times a week with clients, so he told me. At first I believed him, until one day I left work early and went home because I hadn't been feeling well all day."

"When I got home he was there having lunch in our dining room with another woman. He immediately introduced her as his secretary who had just relocated from another state. I took off running in the kitchen, when I ran back in the dining room with a butcher knife they were both gone and the back door was left wide open. Your dad called a couple of hours later and explained to me that he had offered to take his secretary to lunch to welcome her to the firm and to the state of Michigan."

"They stopped by our house because all the lawyers were supposed to go to happy hour that evening and it was already 1:00p.m., so he decided to kill two birds with one stone by going home to shower and make lunch for him and the secretary. It made sense to me, so

I forgave him but I told him to never bring another woman in our home again; I don't care what's going on. He apologized and told me that he would not stay at happy hour for long, and he wanted me to wait up for him, I agreed. After you were sleep for the night, I took a shower and decided that I would read a book and wait for your dad to come home. When I laid my head on the pillow, I smelled a fragrance that your Aunt Connie used to wear. I started sniffing the sheets and that fragrance was all over the sheets as well."

"I started to feel sick to my stomach so I ran into the bathroom to vomit. Right after I threw those sheets in the garbage and put clean ones on the bed, your dad came in. He went to your bedroom and kissed you, and then he came into our bedroom. I confronted him about what I had just found and also of my suspicions, which was that he had sex in our bed with that woman. Of course, he denied having anyone in our bed, but I didn't want to hear it. I told him to take as much of his clothes as he could that night and to get out. We argued back and forth for what seemed like hours."

"I'm not leaving. Not only am I not leaving but I'm

sleeping in our bed with you tonight," Charles yelled. "He said that it had been a long day for us both and that we needed to sleep it off and talk about it in the morning, just like that. My stomach was still upset and now my head was starting to hurt. I did not feel like arguing with him anymore. I took a pillow and blanket and slept on the couch. I woke up seems like shortly after I had fallen asleep to your dad on top of me, I told him to get off, he wouldn't, so I tried to push him off but he was too strong. After I really started fighting to get him off of me, he held me down by my throat and started to rape me. His force was so strong that I passed out."

"When I came to and opened my eyes, he thanked God that I was okay. He had my head propped up on one of the sofa pillows. I told him to take everything that he could fit in his car and leave. I told him that whatever he couldn't take with him would go in the garbage the next morning because I never wanted to see him again."

James Jr., fell to the floor crying hysterically, Mark was also crying.

"Sis I didn't know, I swear," James cried.

"Queen, I told your dad that if he didn't leave I would press rape charges against him which would ruin his career, amongst other things. He never wanted to leave you. I didn't want to tell my family because I knew that your grandfather would probably try to kill him, plus in some weird way, I felt ashamed, like I had done something wrong."

"I was six weeks pregnant at the time. I had a miscarriage the day after the rape. Your father didn't know about the pregnancy. I had just found out myself a couple of days before the incident. We had a dinner planned that weekend just for the two of us and I planned on telling him at the dinner."

Queen had tears streaming down her face; she hugged her mom and whispered in her ear, "Now I get it."

After James picked himself up off the floor, he walked up to Linda and asked for her forgiveness. She grabbed him and hugged him.

"It's already done baby brother, don't worry about it."

James extended his hand to Mark and apologized.

"Mark first of all I want you to know that I am not a racist, maybe an asshole, but definitely not a racist. Also,

I want to thank you for loving my sister and accepting my niece as your own. You're a good man."

"James it takes a big man to admit and apologize for his wrong doing, I appreciate that and I accept your apology," Mark said.

Connie walked into the room and announced that she had just spoken with the doctor and he said that Grandma Beatrice would have a slow recovery and that she would be just fine.

IT'S TIME TO HEAL

"Mark, can you call the firm and take a week off? I would like for us to be here when Momma comes home from the hospital. We're spending Christmas here this year. Connie how about you and I prepare Christmas dinner together like we use to?"

"What am I, mush meat?" James Jr's wife Jackie asked. Connie and Linda both laughed.

"Of course you're not mush meat sis. Me, you, Linda and the girls will all do our part." Connie said.

"Mark I really would like to buy you a drink, that's the least I can do," said James Jr.

"James, I don't drink, but thank you anyway. Your apology was good enough for me man."

After Grandma Beatrice returned home from the hospital, she was surrounded by her large family. She was pleased to have her home filled with so much love. Everyone took their turns waiting on Grandma Beatrice hand and foot.

It was soon time for Linda, Queen and Mark to return home. Everyone hated to see them leave but promised to make plans to get together for the next major holiday. Although so much pain had come from Queens's questions finally being answered, she was so happy to have her family together, everyone enjoying each other. There were lots of laughs and loving going on in that household, so many new memories being made.

A few weeks after Linda returned to California, Grandma Beatrice called Linda to find out how things were going with her and Queenie after the information that was revealed to Queen. Linda told her mom that there was a strain on her and Queenies relationship.

"Momma it hurt me that Queenie found out about her father the way she did. A big part of me was relieved that I finally told her and another part of me was sad because I knew this would hurt her and other people. I vowed to myself that I would never keep any more secrets from her, it's too painful."

"I was trying to protect her, but I think that I've done more harm than good. The last thing I wanted was for Queen to get hurt. She seems a little different these days. I try to get her to talk to me about how she's feeling, but she always says she's okay, but I'm her mom and know that she's not."

"Momma I would really like to get things back the way they were between Queen and me. She's not hostile or disrespectful towards me or anything, there's just a distance between the two of us where there wasn't before. I don't want to push myself on her, I want to give her the space that she needs right now, but at the same time I would like for us to discuss whatever it is that she's feeling."

"Give it some time baby. That was a lot for her to digest. She's been asking for years about the man who loved and adored her so fiercely and to finally find out the reason for him no longer being in her life, I'm sure was very shocking and hurtful. Everything will work itself out. She's going to be okay," Linda's mom said.

"I'm sure it will Momma, I'm just worried about her because we've never been distant with each other."

A New Life

"My doctor recently confirmed that I'm eight weeks pregnant," Linda told her mom. "THAT'S GREAT BABY," Linda's mom yelled.

"Mark will have to spend a lot of time away from me and the new baby because his firm is struggling right now and he's working hard to get things back on track. He and I discussed a possible restructure of the firm; he's going to consider trying a different approach first though. I haven't told Mark about the baby yet. Although he and I discussed expanding our family in the past, I don't know if he's going to be excited or not to find out that we're expecting, seeing as how things are going at his firm."

"Well Linda, I would tell you to take your time, but with this situation you can't. I'm so sorry for everything you and your family have been going through lately. I wish there was something I could do to help you."

"Momma I'm sorry to burden you with my problems, you and Connie have been so good with being there for me and my family."

"Linda listen to me, its okay baby, we're family, you don't have to apologize. We love you, Queen and Mark. We will always be there for you."

"Thanks Momma, I love you so much."

"I love you too Linda."

"Mark, I know that you've been working extra hours trying to get the firm back on track but do you think you can make time to have dinner with Queen and I this evening? I have something important that I would like to discuss with you all."

"Is everything okay baby?" Mark asked.

"Yes, Mark everything is okay, everything is just fine."

"Okay, well I will be home no later than 5:30 this evening, does that work for you?" Mark asked.

"Yes, 5:30 is perfect; Queen should be here around 4:30."

"Well enjoy the rest of your afternoon and call me if you need me, I'm just a phone call away." "I know you are sweetheart and same to you Mark."

Linda prepared her signature bowtie pasta for dinner. She shared her pregnancy news with Queen and Mark, who were both ecstatic. Mark was on cloud nine. Although he raised Queen for most of her life and had considered her as his own daughter, he will now have a biological child of his own. That evening, Christmas came early in the Baskin/Jones household.

Mark explained to Linda that although there's a lot going on at his office, he wanted to take part in everything regarding her pregnancy and she couldn't be happier to hear that. She felt that with everything going on at Mark's office, the news of a baby on the way would add stress to him.

Queen was so happy for her mom and Mark. She hugged them both and told them congrats.

"Mark, I have seen nothing but love between you and my mom. Thank you so much for accepting me as your own, and thank you for adding to my mom's happiness. You have been in my life since I was nine years old and now you get to do it from the beginning. DIAPER CHANGING TIME." yelled Queen.

They all laughed.

"Queen you have made being a father to you easy and it is and has always been my pleasure," Mark said. "You're going to be a great older sister, the perfect role model for your younger sibling."

"I will try my best," Queen said.

The next evening Linda called her mom and her sister Connie to share with them how things went when she told Queen and Mark about her pregnancy.

"Queen had been acting a little different ever since she found out about what happened the night her dad left but last night at dinner she lit up like a light bulb when I told her and Mark about the baby." She also mentioned going away for a few days to Long Beach with some friends in a few weeks."

"Awww, that is so good to hear," Connie said.

"I told you things would be okay Linda." her mom said.

A few weeks later, Mark and Linda went for a prenatal visit. The visit went well. The baby was healthy and developing properly but it was too soon to know what the gender was, which was fine with the expecting parents because they both agreed they didn't want to know. Their only concern was the health of the baby.

Mark was so excited about this baby, he was all in. He signed up for the Lamaze class, prenatal/hospital course and pain management with Linda so that he could help her in whatever way she needed him to. They decided on the colors mint and yellow as the colors for the nursery.

Mark was so overwhelmed with the situation at his office and the news of the baby that he failed to contact his family to share the good news. He had one sister, Charlene (she and her husband had two sons) no brothers and his parents, Allen and Sarah.

"Hi dad, how are things going around there?" Mark asked his father.

"Things couldn't be better Mark. Your mom is still

fattening me up with her cooking."

Mark laughed.

"How are you Mark?' his dad asked.

"I'm just great dad."

"How are Linda and Queen? Is everything okay with them, son?"

"Yes dad, they're both fine."

"That's good to hear Mark."

"Besides checking in with you all, I also wanted to let you know that you will soon be the grandparents of a third grandchild."

"Well it's about time," Allen said. "I'm happy for you and Linda. Your mom is running errands but I'm sure she's going to give you a call once she gets back in."

"Oh okay! I called Charlene to tell her the good news and had to leave a voicemail," Mark said. "Your sister's going to be a proud auntie."

"I know dad. She and I talked about her becoming an aunt a few times."

"I love you kids so much Mark."

"Love you too dad."

Mark was already working hard to get things back on track at his firm and with the addition to the family he knew he needed to either try harder or try something different. With Queen graduating from college soon and them no longer having that bill, Mark wanted to present Linda with the idea of being a stay-at-home mom after the baby comes, but he knew in order for him to do that, he had to make sure all was well at work.

HEART TO HEART

Queen invited Linda out for manicures, pedicures, lunch at Republique, Linda's favorite restaurant and to also do a little shopping for the baby. Queen wanted to buy a few items for her unborn sibling and to also give her mom some special attention.

"Wow Queen, this is so nice. Thank you! We haven't had one of these days in a while." Linda said.

"You're welcome mom. You've been through a lot lately and I just wanted to give you a relaxing day." I also wanted to apologize to you for the way I distanced myself from you after hearing your truth."

"You don't have to apologize baby. I was just concerned about you. You know when you hurt I hurt. I was trying my best to protect you, spare you any pain. I know how much you love and miss your dad but I didn't know how to answer your questions in a way that I felt was gentle. To be honest, I still haven't completely dealt with what happened that night. I don't understand why your father did what he did. It was scary and confusing for me. Over the years, I played back that night over and over in my head, wondering why he felt the need to go that far."

"Mom, I'm so sorry you went through that alone. I think when you told everyone who loves you what you had experienced, the healing process started for you and I both. You're very strong and resilient and I'm proud to have you as my mom."

Linda teared up as Queen spoke.

"Oh, my loving Queenie! I'm so grateful that God chose me to be your mom. I don't know if I would have been this strong woman if I didn't have you. You are so full of love and compassion. You've always kept me on my toes."

"Mom our family is stronger already and we're going to get even stronger. That little bambino you're carrying is the icing on the cake. God has a way of bridging gaps. Had it not been for Grandma Beatrice accident, none of this would have happened."

"What did I do to deserve such an intelligent and insightful daughter?"

"You set the blueprint mom and that's why I'm the way I am."

"I love you Queenie."

"Love you more mom."

A LONG TIME COMING

Over the next few months Linda and Mark enjoyed Linda's pregnancy and getting the nursery ready. Mark strategized about how he was going to turn things around at the firm, thinking about a couple of things he can try.

As Queen was heading out the door on her weekend getaway, she gave her mother a hug.

"Please be safe and have fun Queen," Linda said.

"I most definitely will mom."

Queen drove to LAX airport and boarded a plane to Detroit. That lie Queen told her mom about going to Long Beach was a cover up for her going to Detroit to try and find her father.

Ever since Queen found out about what took place between her parents, she started searching for her father. She searched for him in the past but wasn't able to find him. She started to wonder if he was still alive. She knew her parents met in law school and her dad was a practicing attorney before he left, so she took that information to try and locate him. Prior to Queen going to Detroit she made a list of all the law firms in Detroit and started contacting them.

She called all the firms on her list and then got to the last listing, the woman who answered the phone stated that Charles Jones, no longer worked there.

"Hmmm, he no longer works there?" Queen asked.

"No ma'am, he no longer works here."

Queen introduced herself to the woman on the phone, telling her that she is Mr. Jones daughter and she wanted to know if the woman can provide her with contact information for her father. The woman first stated that she's not allowed to give out that information but then she told Queen that she didn't have any contact information for her dad. Queen felt like the woman did have contact information for her father and maybe if she spoke face to face with this woman, then maybe she would help her out.

Queen arrived at the law firm where the woman said her father no longer works.

"Hi, my name is Queen Jones. I know that my father Charles Jones no longer works here but I would really appreciate it if you would provide me with any contact information you have for him. I'm 22 years old and haven't seen my father since I was 7 years old. I traveled from Los Angeles and will only be here for a few days. I really would like to make contact with him while I'm here. If you don't want to give me contact information for my dad, can I leave my phone number with you to pass on to him, just in case you come across his contact information?"

The woman hesitated for a second before answering Queen with a yes.

"Thank you ma'am," Queen said.

Because Queen's grandparents, aunt and uncle still lived in Detroit, she knew she needed to stay out of sight. She didn't want her family to know that she was searching for her dad. She needed to see him and find out what was going on with him that night he jeopardized his whole family.

She loved and missed her father so much but was also hurt and confused by what her mom described as his actions the last time she saw him.

Queen spent her first day in Detroit holed up in her hotel room, ordering takeout and working on schoolwork. She sent her mom and grandmother a text message to check on them. They were both fine. Queen waited and waited, hoping to hear from her father.

The next morning she worked out in the hotel's fitness room, showered, then went for breakfast in the hotels café.

Queen repeated the same routine from the day before while waiting for a call from her father as she worked on her schoolwork. On her third and final day in Detroit, Queen called her mom that afternoon to check on her. Her mom hadn't been feeling well since the evening before and decided to stay home from work that day. Queen told her mom that she was on her way home and she would see her soon. Queen left Detroit without ever receiving that call from her father.

WE'RE IN THIS TOGETHER

Once Queen made it home she went directly to her mom's bedroom where she saw Linda sleeping. She found Mark in the basement, looking for something in one of the storage areas.

"Hi Mark, how are you doing?" Queen asked.

"I'm well Queen. How was your trip?"

"It was nice. What's going on with my mom?"

"She's been feeling drained and nauseated for the last few days, nothing serious though. Today was actually a better day for her than yesterday was."

"Oh okay! That's nice to hear. Is there anything I can do to help out?" Queen asked.

"Nothing I can think of right now but thanks any way Queen."

Linda felt well enough to return to work the following day. Mark drove to work that morning feeling optimistic that the attorneys he's interviewing today will be a good match. In the last few months, he interviewed a total of seven and felt like it would be in the firm's best interest to keep looking. One of the attorneys was a high profile defense attorney. The other attorney wasn't high profile but he had a very impressive record and reputation.

That evening Mark discussed both candidates with Linda. He was pleased with how the interviews had gone and he knew they had a lot to bring to the table, their credentials were impeccable. He wanted to welcome them both to the firm. Linda reviewed both candidate's credentials and the notes that Mark had jotted down about each individual from the interviews. She agreed with Mark that both men would be a good addition to the firm and encouraged Mark to make them an offer.

It had been two months since both new hires had been working at Mark's firm when Mark and Derek (the high profile attorney) were having lunch. Mark was telling Derek how impressed and appreciative he was with the business he has brought to the firm. Derek mentioned to Mark that Mark's brother-in-law James Jr., had encouraged him to interview with Mark.

Mark stopped eating his food. "James did what?"

Linda never mentioned anything to Mark about this, Mark thought.

"He told me you were looking to add a few attorneys to your firm and he felt like I would be a good fit. After checking out your website, I told James I would keep looking. I wanted to go with a larger firm, which is what I told him. He told me that I would be making a big mistake if I didn't go with you. He spoke highly of you, not only as his sister's husband but as a man and a professional."

Mark was stunned at what he was hearing. "Wow, I didn't expect to hear any of this but I appreciate James's referral and kind words."

After lunch Mark called Linda and told her about the conversation he had with Derek.

"Linda did you know anything about this?"

"No Mark, I didn't know anything about this. I'm

just as surprised as you were. That was very thoughtful of James." Linda said.

"I will give him a call this evening to thank him." Mark said. "Good idea babe. See you soon."

Mark called James that evening and thanked him.

"James, I appreciate what you did for me. Why didn't you tell me you sent Derek?

"I didn't feel it was important for me to tell you. I was just hoping things worked out. I overheard Momma telling Daddy that you were looking to add to your firm and I stuck my nose in again but this time no one got hurt from me doing so."

Mark and James Jr. both laughed. The men talked a bit longer before ending their call.

GREAT MINDS THINK ALIKE

Linda is now seven months along in her pregnancy and is glowing and excited for the newest member of the family to arrive. The nursery was completed a few months ago and she had her baby shower just last month. She was ready.

Mark's firm is in the best shape it's been in in a long time, which gave him the confidence to present the idea to Linda of her becoming a stay-at-home mom after the baby comes.

Linda was sitting at the dining room table when Mark walked in from work.

"Hey honey!" Mark said to Linda.

"Hi babe, how was work today?" Linda said."

"It was very prosperous and smooth sailing, no bumps in the road today."

"That's good to hear," Linda said.

"Well, speaking of work, ever since we've added the newest two attorneys to the firm, things has really looked up."

"Every attorney is doing well but these two have brought in more clients. All of Derek's clients are high profiled, and he's won every case so far, which is why he's so sought after. I was thinking that maybe after the baby is born you can take a break from working, stay-at-home, at least until he or she starts school," Mark said.

Linda started laughing so loud before walking over to Mark. She sat in his lap and gave him a big kiss.

"Great minds think alike babe. Actually, I have a similar thought. I missed a lot of Queen's firsts and cried about missing them. My thought is staying at home until after the baby is potty trained. What do you think about that?" Linda asked.

"That's a good idea as well," said Mark.

"Great! I will record as many of the baby firsts for you as I possibly can."

"Sounds like a plan, honey. I know you and I discussed me taking a month off to help you with the baby but I've decided to take two months off instead," Mark said.

"I'm happy to hear that babe." Linda said.

ROLLERCOASTER OF EMOTIONS

Linda and Queen drove to San Francisco for what would be their last mother and daughter getaway before the baby was born. They had massages, manicures, pedicures, facials and even did some retail therapy. Shortly after they finished having lunch, Linda started feeling sharp pains in her stomach. She sat on a bench for a bit, then started feeling something wet coming from between her legs, which she assumed was her water breaking, but then she saw a look of terror in Queens eyes as Queen cried.

"Mom, I'm going to call 911, we need to get you to a hospital," Queen said as she cried.

Linda was wearing a short dress and decided to look down to see why Queen looked so terrified, that's when she saw drips of blood on the ground and also sliding down her legs.

Linda started to cry. Queen hugged her mom and told her the ambulance was on their way.

While Linda and Queen were in the ambulance, Queen called Mark to let him know the situation and that Linda was being taken to St. Mary's Medical Center.

Once they arrived at the hospital Linda was handed over to a Dr. Jasmine Jones, who immediately started to examine Linda. As Dr. Jones examined Linda, she noticed Linda was still losing blood and had lost quite a bit. She started asking Linda questions in a soothing way as to not upset her any more than she already was.

Dr. Jones went out to the waiting area and explained to Queen that Linda had lost a lot of blood and she's concerned that she might lose the baby. She explained that she's going to give Linda a C-section but they will have to move fast. Queen told the doctor that Mark was on his way there by plane and should be there soon. After Dr. Jones explained to Linda what her plan was, the nurses moved forward with prepping Linda for her C-section.

While Queen sat nervously in the waiting area, a man went to the nurse's station asking if his wife is still there. He explained that he had come to pick his wife up but she hadn't come out. "Mr. Jones, Dr. Jones is performing an emergency C-section, she should be finished soon," the nurse said.

"Oh okay!" When she's finished, can you let her know that I'm waiting for her in the lounge area," the man said. As Queen listened to this conversation, she was thinking to herself how familiar that voice sounded.

About five minutes after Dr. Jones husband walked away, Mark came rushing in the waiting area. Queen explained to Mark more in details as to what took place prior to Linda being taken to the hospital and also about the C-section.

They both waited a short while before the doctor came out and told them that Linda and their baby boy was doing fine and Linda was being taken to the prenatal unit. Mark and Queen cried and hugged.

"When can we see them" Queen asked excitedly.

"Once they're taken to the prenatal unit and settled, you will be able to see them. If you'd like, I can have the nurse let you know when you can go see them."

"That would be much appreciated," Mark said.

Mark and Queen both thanked the doctor for taking care of Linda and the baby. Queen told Mark that she will be right back; she was going to the gift shop.

Queen asked the nurse at the nursing station for directions to the lounge area.

As Queen was entering the lounge area, she saw Dr. Jones talking to her husband, and observed the doctor telling her husband that she will be right back. Queen stood there for a minute watching the doctor's husband as he watched the television on the wall. She then walked up to him and asked him if his name was Charles Jones. The man answered her with a yes.

"Are you from Detroit, Michigan?" Another yes, "do you have a daughter named Queen Jones?" The man stood up, staring at Queen in disbelief, tears started streaming down his face. "Yes I do!"

They both just stood there crying, not talking, not hugging. Charles finally held his arms out and Queen stepped up as he grabbed her close to him.

Just then Dr. Jones returned to the lounge area with her purse and bag.

"Charles, what's going on, who's this?" she asked.

"Jasmine, this is my daughter, Queen."

As Queen cried, she told her dad how Jasmine saved her baby brother. Charles looked even more confused as he did when Queen had approached him. Although he hadn't been in touch with Linda in years, hearing about her giving birth was a shocker for him but Queen and Linda being in San Francisco was even more confusing. He had missed so much of their lives. After she explained the whole ordeal, Queen and Linda being in San Francisco made more sense to him now. Queen explained to Charles how she recently had gone to Detroit searching for him at the law firm. He was stunned but happy to know that she thought about him just as much as he thought about her.

"Dad, we need to talk, I have questions," Queen said.

"I'm sure you do baby and we will talk and I will answer any questions you have, I owe you that."

Queen told her dad that she needed to go see about

her mom and new little brother. They exchanged numbers and embraced each other again.

"I love you dad and I will call you soon."

"I love you too baby and I look forward to hearing from you."

Queen didn't know when and how she was going to tell her mom that she had seen her dad or even tell her mom the identity of the doctor who had delivered her baby but she knew now wasn't a good time for that conversation. Queen hurried to the gift shop to buy a gift for her mom and her baby brother before heading back to the waiting area with Mark.

Strengthened Bonds

While Queen was perusing the Hallmark cards looking for a nice card for her mom, she ran across a 'congratulations dad' card. She purchased the congratulations dad card for Mark and wrote a message in it, which read, "Congratulations dad on your new bundle of joy. Thank you for always being there for mom and me. Thank you for showing up and showing out for the good and bad times. Thank you for never making me feel like your stepchild but like I was your biological daughter. Thank you for telling me NO but also saying but this is what I will do, which always turned out to be what was best for me. Simply put, thank you for being you."

Queen was so excited to have reconnected with her

father but she had no plans on treating Mark any differently than she had always treated him.

As Queen was writing her message in Mark's card, she teared up, thinking about what had taken place earlier with her mom, her finally seeing her dad after all of these years and just being grateful her mom and baby brother were both safe and healthy. She went in the bathroom to clean her face before heading back to the waiting area.

She approached Mark in the waiting area and gave him a hug. As Mark looked at Queen, he could tell that she had been crying. Confused, Mark asked, "Queen are you okay, did something happen?"

As Queen handed Mark the card, she told him that she was okay. Mark read the card and instantly teared up. He and Queen hugged.

"Queen, I could not have asked for a better daughter. Having you in my life has made me a better man and made me want to experience fatherhood from birth. You are and have always been so thoughtful, caring and mature. Your mom and I always have conversations about how proud of you we are. Grandma Sarah,

Grandpa Allen and your Aunt Charlene adore you for all the reasons your mom and I are proud of you." Mark said.

"Thank you Mark! I just wanted to let you know that I appreciate you. Can we go see mom now?"

"Yes, we can, I was waiting for you to come back" said Mark.

Queen and Mark took turns holding the baby; Queen took selfies of her and her baby brother and lots of photos of her mom, Mark and the baby and sent them to Grandma Beatrice. Mark sent photos to his mom, dad and sister. Queen stood back, watching her mom and Mark with their new baby. They both were so happy and she was just as happy as they were, especially with finally seeing her dad. Queen had planned on calling Grandma Beatrice when they got back home and telling her about the encounter she had with her dad. She'd never asked her grandmother to keep a secret for her but she would this time. Queen needed someone that she could confide in because she had to tell someone. She was so happy and wanted to share that with someone. She knew that her grandmother would be happy for her. Queen felt that everything was coming full circle for her family. She was finally getting her whole family back.

A Good Ole Talking

Caleb Anthony Baskin is what Linda and Mark named their son. It's been two months since Caleb's arrival and the new parents have had very little sleep but they don't care, Caleb is their pride and joy. Mark's returning to work in the next few weeks and his family is coming to visit within the next few days before he goes back. Queens's family is going to visit the baby the month after Marks family, they decided to wait so that Mark can spend time with his family before returning to work, plus they didn't want Linda and Mark to be overwhelmed with out of town family.

Queen had been so occupied with school, work and helping Mark and her mom out that she failed to call grandma Beatrice more sooner than later.

"Hello Grandma Beatrice, is now a good time to talk"?" Queen asked her grandmother.

"Yes baby, I just finished cleaning the house. Now is the perfect time to talk. How are things going around there since your baby brother's arrival?" Grandma Beatrice asked.

"It's definitely different. I have to share mom now. We don't have a lot of one on one time together anymore but I'm totally fine with it. Caleb is so adorable, and he knows my voice already. He grips my finger every time I hold him." Queen said.

"That's sweet Queenie. He knows big sister is going to be his protector," Grandma Beatrice said.

"That's for sure grandma. I can't wait to see you all next month," Queen said. "I'm excited to see you all as well my baby. I can't wait to give you a big kiss and to hold and kiss that little Caleb," said grandma.

"How's Grandpa James?" Queen asked her grandmother. "Your grandfather is fine baby. He has been helping your Aunt Connie and them with some home renovations," said Grandma Beatrice.

"Oh, that's nice of him," Queen said.

"Grandma, a few months before my mom gave birth to Caleb I went to Detroit looking for my dad."

"Queen Jones you did what?" Grandma Beatrice asked.

"I went to the law firm my dad used to work at looking for him but the receptionist claimed to have not had any contact information for him," Queen said.

"Your mother never mentioned this to me, does she know you went?" Grandma Beatrice asked. "No, she doesn't know, yet. I plan on telling her but with her being pregnant I felt it wasn't a good time to tell her before I went. I don't know how she would have felt about that. I don't know how she would have reacted. I didn't want to cause her any stress," Queen said.

"Well that's understandable Queenie but the baby has been here for a few months now, when exactly do you plan on telling her?" Grandma Beatrice asked.

"There's more grandma," Queen said.

"Oh really!" grandma said.

"Yes ma'am" Queen said.

"The doctor that delivered Caleb is my biological dad's wife. I saw my dad at the hospital while my mom was having her C-section. He had come to the hospital to pick his wife up and while he was waiting for her, I approached him," Queen said.

"Wow Queenie, this is better than them soap operas I be watching," Grandma Beatrice said. "Did you have to tell him who you were or he knew," grandma asked.

"He knew," said Queen.

"Wow! So you've been very busy I see. How are you feeling, did you two get a chance to talk, did he say anything to you about the last time he saw you?" grandma asked.

"We have not talked yet. We've sent a few text messages back and forth. I told him I would call him. He knows I have questions and have agreed to answer any questions I have," said Queen.

"Well I'm happy to hear that," grandma said.

"Grandma Beatrice…"

"Yes Queen" grandma said. "Prior to my mom telling all of us about what happened that night between she and my dad, did you know?" Queen asked.

"No baby, I had no idea your mom had gone through any of that and it crushed my heart knowing that my baby went through that alone and carried that secret with her for so many years," grandma said.

"I know what you mean Grandma Beatrice. I feel the same way as you. Her tearing up almost every time I would ask her about my dad's whereabouts and why he was no longer in our lives all made sense when she explained to us what happened that night. She told me that she still hadn't dealt with what happened that night. She said she didn't understand why my dad had gone so far. When I talk with my dad, I need him to explain everything to me. I need to know, not only for myself, but for mom as well. Maybe if she can make sense as to why my dad did what he did, then she will have the closure that she deserves," Queen said.

"Well I hope once she finds out, that closure will be the only result of her finding out." Grandma Beatrice said.

"What do you mean granny?" Queen asked.

"What I mean is, your mom went through something traumatic that night and as a result of what she went through, she lost her baby. I do believe that knowing exactly what was on your dad's mind that night will give her closure but on the other hand, it can possibly cause her more emotional distress. That's the last thing I want for her period but especially now sense she has

Caleb to care for and be strong for," Grandma said.

"Oh okay, I got it granny," said Queen.

"Grandma Beatrice can you please keep this conversation between the two of us. I haven't told anyone else about my dad and his wife."

"Sure baby, I won't say anything," grandma said.

"Thank you granny!"

I TAKE FULL RESPONSIBILITY

Queen had mixed feelings about hearing her father's side of the story. Although she wanted to know what happened, hearing about the horrible ordeal her mom experienced that night, she was very curious as to what her dad is going to say. And after the conversation she had with her grandmother she was kind of having second thoughts about ever mentioning to her mom whatever her father says or even mentioning seeing him.

As Queen was returning home from work, Linda and Mark were leaving out with baby Caleb to run some errands. Queen decided now would be a perfect time to talk with her dad; she had put it off long enough.

"Hi dad, how are you doing?" Queen asked Charles.

"I'm well Queen. How are you?" Charles said.

"Well dad, I'm working towards finishing up this last semester strong before I graduate," said Queen.

"That's good to hear daughter, I'm so proud of you."

"Thanks daddy. So, how long have you and Jasmine been married?"

"Jasmine and I have been married for five years."

"Oh, how long have you lived in San Diego and is that where you and Jasmine met?"

"I've lived in San Diego for nine years and yes, Jasmine and I met here in San Diego."

"Do you all have any children?"

"No children for us. We've tried for years but nothing has happened."

"I'm sorry to hear that daddy. Something will happen one day."

"Thank you Queenie and I'm hoping it will," said Charles.

"Dad, what happened between you and mom the night you left?"

"I was a big fool that night Queen. I was a new attorney. I had a great start to my career, great peers, great family, everything was going really well. I couldn't have asked for any more than what I had, because I had everything I needed and wanted. Your mom and I had been talking about adding a new baby to the family. We didn't want you to grow up without having a sibling and you were already seven years old at that time. When I would bring up the subject every now and then, it seemed as though she was trying to put me off. One of the times she told me to stop pressuring her. She said that if it happens it happens. I never felt like I was pressuring her but I did feel like she had changed her mind about us adding to the family. We weren't using protection but she also hadn't gotten pregnant either, so I felt that she was probably using some form of birth control."

"There were so many thoughts going on in my mind. I loved your mom and the family and life we had created but I felt betrayed. We had always had respect for each other and great communication."

"I started spending quite a bit of time after work with some of my peers, which your mom made it very clear she wasn't comfortable with. I told her it was work related just to keep her off my back but I really just wanted some time to think. I needed to make sure that these feelings of betrayal I was having was not my imagination because like I said, your mom and I had always had a great relationship, good communication but I just felt like something was different."

"A secretary had been hired for me. She had just re-located to Detroit. Sometimes after work she would go to happy hour with us. One day I was telling her and a few others about how great the food and service was at a restaurant that had just opened a few blocks from our office. A few days after this conversation, she asked me a few specifics about the restaurant. I offered to take her there for lunch the next day but I didn't do my planning really well because the same day I was supposed to have taken her to lunch we had a special happy hour going on that same evening. One of the other attorneys was about to become a dad for the first time so we were to celebrate with him."

"Instead of me giving the secretary a rain check for the lunch date I promised her, I asked her to run home with me so that I can shower and then make us a quick lunch. I was pressed for time. One thing led to another and we had sex in me and your mom's bed. It wasn't planned; I've never cheated on your mom before. Your mom unexpectedly came home because she wasn't feeling well that day at work. According to her, she was going to come home and lay down for a few hours before it was time for her to pick you up. When she came in, I was preparing our lunch and your mom rightfully so got angry when she saw this woman in our dining room. I left with the woman, went back to work. I called your mom from the office and apologized and tried calming her down. I lied and told her nothing was going on between the other woman and me. I told her about me not planning my day well which led me to try and kill two birds with one stone by showering and making lunch for the secretary and me. I asked her to wait up for me so that we can talk about it, she agreed."

"I had one too many to drink that night and caught a cab home. When I got home your mom clearly had found evidence that I had lied earlier about nothing happening between the secretary and me. She was furious with me. We argued, did a lot of yelling. She banned me from the bedroom but I refused to leave so she left and slept on the couch. When I was in our bedroom alone I started to think about the event I had just left, celebrating a colleague as being a first time dad. I thought about what I felt was a situation with your mom and I and us adding to our family and her no longer wanting to. I went downstairs where she was sleeping on the couch and started having sex with her, she didn't want it and told me to get off of her but I didn't. She tried fighting me off of her, when she did that I put my arms around her throat to try and subdue her but I went too far and choked her, to until she had passed out. I don't have an excuse or reason for what I did to your mom that day with my secretary and that night when I returned from the celebration."

"When she came to, she told me to leave and she never wanted to see me again. I left liked she asked me to. I was so hurt and embarrassed for everything I had done to our family. I couldn't think of a way to make it right. A week after the incident, I sought therapy. I needed to make sense of what I had done. All of my actions that day were out of character for me. The therapist I worked with felt like along with me feeling betrayed by my wife, celebrating another man adding to his family, the amount I had drank that night and my quick rising star in the law firm, that I had become full of myself and probably felt entitled to this child that your mom and I discussed both wanting. She said that maybe I was pressuring your mom and hadn't realized it, causing your mom frustration….which is a big possibility."

"The therapist felt like based on what I told her I felt like your mom wasn't ready for a second child like she had told me and maybe I had some resentment towards her for that reason causing me to erupt that night. After thinking about it, what the therapist said made a lot of sense. I regretted not talking to your mom more about the situation as opposed to assuming. I was very wrong and had never been like that with your mom before."

"I didn't know how to fix it. I never wanted to be apart from you and your mom. Shortly after my therapy ended I relocated to San Diego. I did not want to run into your mom. What I did to her that night was very traumatic for her. I had always been our family protector. Never in a million years would I have guessed I would have been someone to inflict pain on his own family. I had a lot of soul searching and maturing to do. Queen, I take full responsibility for not being a part of your life, I'm sorry baby."

"Thank you dad," Queen said.

"Dad, at the time of the incident between you and mom, she was six weeks pregnant and was going to tell you at the dinner you all had planned that weekend. The morning after the incident, she had a miscarriage."

Queen could hear her father crying on the other end of the phone. She cried along with him. "Dad, I'm going to go now but I will call you another day. I love you."

"I love you too Queen." Queen knew her father needed to process what she had just told him about Linda's miscarriage and she needed to process all of what he had just told her. After disconnecting from her father, Queen sat there thinking for a moment. Her father's reasoning for acting a fool with her mom was because he felt like she didn't want any more children with him but it was right there the whole time and he messed it up. If her father knew this, he would probably be kicking himself in the butt more than he already has.

FINALLY SOME CLOSURE

Queen wanted to share this information with her mom in hopes of her mom finally being able to understand her father's thought process behind what he had done, which will hopefully lead to closure for her mom but there was so much more to tell her. She still hadn't told Linda about the identity of the doctor who had delivered baby Caleb nor that her father was at the hospital.

Caleb is now five months old and Queen, Linda, Mark and baby Caleb was taking their first family photo of four today, afterwards Linda and Queen were going to hang out together for a little while and Mark was going to take the baby home with him because he had some work to catch up on. This will be Linda and

Queen's first time having some girl time since before the baby was born.

Queen had given it a lot of thought and felt as if she should tell her mom everything regarding her dad. Just like Linda was trying to protect Queen's feelings by not telling her the situation surrounding her father no longer being a part of their lives, Queen was trying to protect her mom feelings by not telling her mom everything. The more time had passed, the more Queen started to understand more and more how her mom must have loved her so much that she felt it was in Queen's best interest to not tell her what she had been asking for years.

After Linda and Queen's facials were done they went for lunch.

"Mom, how have you been feeling since Caleb's birth?" Queen asked her mom.

"I feel relaxed knowing I don't have to hand Caleb over to a sitter while I go off to work. I'm going to start back working out in the next few weeks. I love my job but I don't miss it at all. I love being there for lil man."

"That's good to hear. You seem so happy and relaxed." Queen said.

"I am baby. You all make me so happy," said Linda.

After this conversation with her mom, Queen knew telling her mom would be okay. Her mom is still the strong and resilient woman she had known her mom to be. She can handle it.

"Mom, do you ever think about my dad?" Queen asked her mom.

"Not at all, I hope things are going well for him but he's not someone that's ever on my mind." "If you ever seen him again and he apologized, how do you think you would react? Would you be accepting of his apology? Queen asked her mom.

"I don't know Queen; this isn't something I've ever thought about. Why the talk about your dad all of a sudden.

"Two months before Caleb was born, when I told you I was spending a few days with some friends, I really went to Detroit to find my dad."

Linda sat up straight in her chair looking sternly at Queen.

"Queen, what do you mean you went looking for your dad and why am I just finding out about this?" Linda asked.

"Ever since you told us about your ordeal with dad I've wanted to know what would drive him to do something like that. I didn't understand why he would hurt you. He had always loved and took care of us. I don't think I had ever seen him angry. I had questions for him mom. Stressing you out was the last thing I wanted to do, you were pregnant. Plus, I didn't know what he would tell me and part of me didn't want to open old wounds and the other part was hoping to be able to give you closure since you said you hadn't completely dealt with what happened that night."

"I wasn't quite sure I would tell you but I wanted to know. The Charles Jones you described from that night was not Charles Jones I remember." Queen said.

"Oh baby! I just wish you would have told Mark and me." "Did you see him and did your grandmother and granddad know anything about this?" Linda asked Queen.

"I found the law firm he had last worked for but he no longer worked there and they didn't have any contact information for me. Grandma Beatrice and Grandpa James didn't know anything about this at the time."

"At the time? Linda asked.

"I told Grandma Beatrice about it months after I had gone and asked her not to tell anyone. Mom, please don't be upset with her."

"Queen, I'm not upset with your grandmother. I know how close you two are." Babe, if you ever do anything like that again, please let me know."

"Mom there won't be a next time."

"Oh good Queen" said Linda.

"I saw my dad already," said Queen.

"Wait, what?" said Linda.

"I saw my dad at the hospital you delivered Caleb in." Queen said.

"What are you talking about Queen?" Linda asked.

"Dr. Jones, the doctor that delivered Caleb is my dad's wife."

Linda was shocked and sat in silence for a little while.

"What else Queen, is there anything else you would like to tell me?" Linda asked.

"My dad came to pick Dr. Jones up from the hospital while I was sitting in the waiting area. I didn't see his face but I heard his voice, which sounded very familiar to me. Dr. Jones was still in the delivery room with you so my dad told the nurse if she could let Dr. Jones know he would be waiting for her in the lounge area. After Mark arrived, I went to the lounge area to see if the familiar voice I heard was actually my dad, like I thought it was."

"Wait, so does Mark know about this?" Linda asked.

"No mom, only Grandma Beatrice knows.

"I didn't have the conversation that day with my dad because, well you know, you and Caleb were more important. I recently called him and we talked. To make a long story short, him acting a fool towards you was a combination of things, mainly him feeling like you really didn't want to have another child with him like you all discussed, paired with him celebrating another man becoming a new father (something he wanted) and him having too much to drink that night. He felt so remorseful that he sought counseling the week after the incident and once his counseling was completed, he relocated to San Diego, which is where he met Dr. Jones. They don't have any children but have tried with no success. He didn't want you two to run into each other. He didn't know how to make things right so he felt like that was the least he could do. I told him about you being pregnant and losing the baby, he didn't take it too well. I haven't spoken with him since."

"Wow Queen, that's a lot. What's most important is that you're safe and you got what you were looking for," Linda said.

"Mom, I got what WE were looking for. I hope that what I've just told you will help with your healing and give you closure."

"Thank you baby and I love you so much."

"Love you too mom."

"Mom, can I ask a huge favor?" Queen said.

"Sure anything sweetheart," Linda said.

"I'm sure you will need some time to think about this but will you please consider giving my dad the opportunity to apologize to you?" Queen said.

"You're right Queen, I will need some time to think about that and honestly speaking, I don't need an apology. What you've shared with me today was more than enough," Linda said.

"I understand mom but the apology would be more

for my dad than for you. He was very embarrassed and hurt by his actions. I just want him to be able to apologize. He did the work on himself which is the therapy he mentioned and he also took full accountability." Queen said.

"I understand baby. I will let you know." Linda said.

Not only did Queen want the same closure for her dad that she and her mom now had, but her father had already missed so much of her life that she was thinking it would be nice to have him at her college graduation. Although Charles suffering was his own doing, Queen felt like he had suffered enough and him apologizing to Linda and starting to rebuild his relationship with Queen will help him on his healing path.

That night Linda laid in bed thinking about everything Queen had revealed to her. She thought about poor Queen and what she must be feeling. To have her father be her everything as a young girl to him disappearing out of her life for years with no explanation then as a young adult to find out from her mom the surprising and sickening reason for his disappearance, Queen sneaking and traveling out of state to find her father to get answers, to running into her dad at the hospital her mom was having an emergency delivery, to finding out that the kind and nurturing doctor who delivered her baby brother was her father's wife. Wow.... Linda thought. That's a lot for any person to go through but to know that her daughter has been suffering ever since her father left and longing for not only to have him as a part of her life again but to find out the reason behind why he did what he did to her mom. Her baby had been going through a lot.

Thinking about all of this kept Linda tossing and turning for most of the night. Right when she started to snooze off, baby Caleb started crying. After Linda changed and fed the baby she sat in the rocking chair, rocking him back to sleep, next thing she knew, Mark was waking her up. A few hours had passed since Linda had gone into the nursery. After Mark put the baby in his crib he and Linda went back to their bedroom.

Linda laid in Mark's arms and cried as she told him everything that Queen had revealed to her, that Queen wanted her to hear Charles out and allow him to apologize and that Queen would also like Charles to attend her college graduation. Linda had dumped so much on Mark that he literally was speechless initially.

"I want to hear Charles out and accept his apology, like Queen wants me to, but just thinking about that night stirs up anger in me all over again. Mark, although I've tried for years to block that night out, I've never been able to. Each and every time Queen would ask me about Charles, it brought back memories of that night and tears would start to form in my eyes. It took a lot for me to hold back from crying. I didn't want Queen to see me crying. How can I forgive him for such an unimaginable heinous act? So unimaginable that I could never bring myself to telling our daughter why her daddy was no longer a part of our lives. Ugh, that damn Charles. I was his wife, his child's mother, his best friend. How could he? ESPECIALLY, after I said no. That bastard!" said Linda.

"He wants to be forgiven. He has no idea how much pain and anxiety he's caused me. Because of him I lost our baby. Because of him, our daughter spent her younger years constantly asking and wondering where her father was, then her teen years and as a young adult." Linda said. Just as Linda was about to continue on with her rant, she heard baby Caleb on the baby monitor making cooing sounds. She slowly started to calm from her anger.

"You know Mark, although I'm pissed with Charles, I do realize had it not been for his actions that night, there would be no Caleb. After Queen found out what her father had done to me that night, she was disgusted, angry and just as confused as I was as to why he had acted the way he did that night and she got her answer after she talked with him and was even able to forgive him. All Queen asked of me is to hear her father out and accept his apology. Knowing how she suffered without her father, this isn't asking a lot of me. Queen is my heart. Why wouldn't I do whatever I can to make her life even happier? I don't want my anger to get in the way of her having a relationship with her father." Linda said.

"That explains the sadness in Queens's eyes at the hospital. I thought the tears were about the ordeal you had just experienced," Mark told Linda.

"Mark I think it's a combination of all of this mess weighing heavy on my baby," Linda said.

"Linda, I think you should hear your ex-husband out

and support Queen in inviting him to her graduation. That's my opinion but I will support you in whatever you decide," said Mark.

"Baby, I've been up most of the night thinking about this and have decided that I will talk to Charles and hear him out. He made an awful mistake and from what Queen has told me, he feels remorseful, he's taken full responsibility, identified where he went wrong and he's admittedly worked on himself. He deserves forgiveness and closure, plus, this is Queens's father and she has nothing to do with what happened. Her and her dad is supposed to be in each other's lives. Actually, I need a bit of forgiveness myself, because I should have thought of a better way to handle this situation so that Queen would have not had to wonder for years about her father's whereabouts but I was struggling myself baby. I was so confused. Charles and I had many years of history way before Queen was even thought of and he has never been violent to me or anyone. I didn't know where his actions were coming from and why he went so far." Linda said.

"Well baby, forgiving yourself and Charles will be good for everyone involved. Everyone now has clarity and can move on with the healing process."

"And that's a good feeling Mark," Linda said.

FAMILY TREE COMPLETED

Queen's graduation was fast approaching and her mom still hadn't given her an answer as to if she would be willing to accept an apology from her dad. She had spoken with her dad briefly a few times since the conversation she had with her mom regarding him but she hadn't yet mentioned that she wanted to invite him to her graduation. If her mom wasn't ready to talk with him, she felt it would be inappropriate to invite him…. it would be too awkward.

Queen and Linda were shopping for a graduation outfit for Queen.

"Mom, if you're not willing to accept an apology from my dad I will respect that but just wondering if you had given it any though," Queen said.

"Yes Queen, I've given it plenty of thought and I will talk with your dad and hear him out. It's time for us to do this so that we can all hopefully put this behind us." Linda said.

With a huge smile on her face, Queen said, "You're a rock star mom."

"Nope Queenie, that's all you, my wise and busy daughter."

"You're the one who raised me," Queen said.

They laughed and hugged.

"Oh! One more thing mom," Queen said.

"Now what Queen, what is it?" Linda asked.

"After you and dad talk, I would like to invite him to my graduation."

"That's already taken care of on this end. I talked to your grandmother and grandfather about everything and I strongly and obviously correctly, assumed that you would want to invite him to your graduation. Your grandfather is still coming here with the rest of the family but has agreed to stay at the house and give your dad his ticket," Linda said.

Even if Linda didn't want to do this for Charles, she knew that she needed to do it for Queen. Queen had invested so much time in trying to find her father and in trying to get closure for them all. Why wouldn't she do this for her and Charles' daughter?

Queen was so excited to hear that her mom was open to not only an apology but Linda was one step ahead of her in making sure there was a ticket for Queens's graduation for her dad.

Queen had set up a time for her mom and dad to talk. Charles called Queen's cell phone and Linda answered.

"Hello," Linda said.

"Hi Linda, it's Charles, how are you doing?"

"I'm well Charles, thank you for asking."

"Linda, first of all thank you so much for doing such a great job at raising our daughter. She's something else. I'm very proud of her, of both of you all." Charles said.

"Yes, she's something else alright and thank you, Charles." Linda said.

"I'm sorry for what I did to you and ultimately what I did to Queen, our family." I was being selfish and unreasonable. I wasn't thinking clearly and started wanting things MY way instead of sticking to how you and I had always been with each other, a team. Please believe me when I tell you that I paid the price. Not only with losing the two people who meant the most to me in this world but I paid in other ways as well and I deserved it all. I've learned and I've grown a lot. If I could take back what I did, I would but all I have to offer is an apology and ask for your forgiveness," Charles said.

"Charles thank you for this and the forgiveness was already done before you and I started this conversation." Linda said.

"Thank you, Linda," Charles said.

"You're welcome Charles, and Queen would like for you to come to her graduation in a few weeks. There's a ticket for you. I will give her the phone and she can give you the details. Take care Charles," said Linda.

Queens's graduation day was here, and she was glowing. She had her parents, both sets of grandparents, aunts, uncles and cousins there for her. She didn't have enough tickets for everyone to attend the graduation but everyone was going to join in for the celebration at her house, which would go into the weekend.

Queen decided not to invite her dad to their home for the celebration because Uncle James, who didn't attend the graduation but was at Queen's house with the other family members weren't as forgiving as Queen's mom. That's another situation that is going to take some time and a lot of doing to fix, but for now, Queen was just happy to have her family together again.

At one point she stood back in the cut holding baby Caleb and just watching her family interact, laugh, and enjoy each other's company, making more memories. Her family tree was now complete.

About the Author

Athalia Monae is a Chicago native, author, and entrepreneur. She's been writing and journaling for years. Several years ago, she wrote a short story for a magazine contest but missed the online submission by two minutes. Over the years many people who've read her story have encouraged her to publish it, which inspired Athalia to write *Why the Secrets.*